Table of Contents

Orthodox Britain

***

Audrius Razma

Legal Notice

It's an art of fiction never intended to be a resemblance of living but create an alternative reality parallel to our lives, helping us experience a sensation and entertainment of non-existing events.

If the coincidental information about fictitious forms of work comes into mind, they never intended it to mention neither living nor dead from reality.

The copyright is solely of the author or is otherwise stated. With any misuse of the information and creative works, one will be liable for its actions.

Acknowledgements

In the memory of Prince Philip we will take a last ride. The most sincere condolences, let him rest in peace and shine in our memories.

We would also like to appreciate master filmmakers Takeshi Kitano and Guy Richie.

We must remember our godfather of horror movies Rob Zombie, who made a new trend forbidding major actors to survive his thrilling silver screen.

Let's see these twists of fortune capture our imagination.

Author expresses sincere thank you for the Cartels Writers group allowing him to grow and learn to be a writer.

Let's compliment Prowritingaid writing partners in crime.

Manifesto

Three weeks from now prison gates bangs and our Ignacius and Simon are walking into the prison van.

They have just been found guilty of double homicide and they look in awful spirits from the decision in the crown courthouse.

Simon, "Well it was well knowing you Ignacius" he has a black eye and large patch on his chest starting in a middle black going to blue and ending in a yellow circle from the prison beating he had when guards were taking him to court.

Ignacius smiles with a swollen jaw, "I wonder how long it will take before the dentist."

Simon sits in a prison van seat while they park it in the courthouse garage and leans back, "Where the hell is our Mage", he thinks to himself.

Then the prison escort receives the green light to leave the gates and starts its engine. The two prison van guards are heading off, the guard on the passenger seat takes out a bottle of still water from the glove compartment and takes the lid off, he pours the water in his mouth and swallows it, "We have another duty on route, anyway mate it is a pleasure to meet you. I can see you are our new guy here".

The driver takes a turn to Pimlico Street and while he is watching the rear mirror, he can see the guy sitting in blue and white uniform is closing his eyes to slide asleep near the door window, "a pleasure to meet you, I am Mage".

While, across the river where Prison van is heading is Gothminster House of Island Nation. The highest Lord of the House is relaxing in front of his window overlooking the green river. He is thinking to complete and sign executive law paper he is an architect behind the order. The Lord is sitting in red ox blood colour seat made from wooden frame. He places his left arm on carved Demon head before he seals the executive order. He takes off paperwork from red leather table top and leaves it in a red suitcase to hear a knock on his office door, "Your Excellency we are ready to have lunch time", he takes his gaze away from sunshine and takes a sharp look at his attendant, "I am ok to have lunch in office because I need to sign more orders", young attendant replies, "Yes your Excellency David".

A while later the lunch servant walks in to show today's food options and while he is showing the lunch menu to the Excellency, he places his old tired hand in his pocket to pull out his shoelace. He grabs his Excellence on his neck and pulls tight. The executive chair swings from side to side making silent squeaks but he is holding with his knee to make Lord of Gothminster lose his ground on his chair while he is grasping for his air, "I think one rat is done".

***

Ignacius inspects around him and asks Simon where are they taking us while the prison van is heading now in a forest, Simon "I think we are now fugitives running from court cases".

Ignacius, "I would love to have my kebab now."

Simon smiles and licks his lips, "Do you know a good joke about lawyers?".

Ignacius, "I had enough of this law today, you just keep it down."

Simon, "The government lawyers are the law brokers who sell the law and lawyers are those who protect the law."

Ignacius, "I would not mind meeting these brokers to break their bones."

Simon, "I am sure your time comes same as everyone's,"

Ignacius, "good", he shows a thumb up.

***

When Ignacius was thinking about having his fast food on the other side of Crimson Island, the Dark Lord is giving a good beating in his basement to his tied up in chair Foreign Excellency Blond. While Vice Excellency is watching she is feeling tempted by his majesty's supreme powers in a corner and she then craves to offer herself to him, she passes him a towel to wipe blood off his hands. Then she places one hand on FE Blond shoulder and pulls up her office skirt to show the Dark Lord she is not wearing underneath, "o our supreme Lord commander I want you as much as did our Blond, I am sure Mr Blond won't mind it".

He pulls his pants off after he throws a bloody towel on the side of the floor, "I understand you do not love to fail".

Dark Lord takes her waist closer, stretching her to ramp in her backside while she is still holding her hand on her Foreign Excellency shoulders.

***

The twin sisters from Japan have arrived at Crimson Nation Island. Their names were Nami and Yami Suki. They handed their passports and smiled, "Arigato!!", then they took a cab from Central Airport to their Five-Star Hotel suite. The hotel was not far from the Crimson Island Capital tourist spots to enjoy walking street districts.

They were here for romantic dating holidays to find holiday romance while they conduct their original business trip plans.

When Nami is in a shower, Yami is looking out their twin bedroom window into the street lights replacing their daylight, she could see her reflection in the window, making her know she is just as good as her sister.

They had agreed only to one difference: to have ponytail hair and Nami to style piggy tail on her hair.

She can hear the bathroom door open and her sister walks in, only holding her towel. Nami walks closer to her and whispers in her ear, "I still left the shower room all hot and steamy for you, here take my towel or you just would like me to be with me if you wish so, hehehe."

Yami shrugs her shoulders and shakes her head side to side, holding her lips tucked together, "I want my shower too".

Nami smiles, takes a seat on her bed and throws her wet towel on Yami's shoulder, "You better have fun", she crosses her naked legs together. Yami grabs the towel off her shoulder and walks away, feeling in a rush. She walks in the shower room and before she takes a good wash, she takes off her white t-shirt and folds it in a square.

Yami reaches for her black linen trousers buttons and has them off to fold it square next to her t-shirt. With a touch of a finger D Cup bra drops from front of her chest to let her breast slide while she is still holding on her white satin bra, "gosh it was long day and I feel like soaking in today", she says to herself and she folds it in half to place it on her t-shirt.

Yami slaps her butt check while looking at herself in a mirror and takes off her underwear.

The shower curtain pulls wide open, and she walks in the shower, "I hope my lovely sister has not done you dead mister pervert?", in the shower is a lying man. He is bleeding and held together on a single rope.

He is gasping for air through Nami's tucked-in underwear in his mouth and his arms with legs up backwards together making him arch. The rope continues around his neck and over shower curtain rail.

Yami smile and sits on his butt naked making her so small compared to Caucasian man in his 60s with grey hair on his head. Her soft hand brushes over his cheeks for him to close his eyes, "do not worry I have my turn to have my dinner first, she left me for you", she can see him bleeding from short stab wounds around his abdominal sides in three to four places with non-vital stabs.

The curtains close and she adjusts tap water to favourite temperature before she turns on the shower, "about time for my blood bath", steps on with strength on his wounds to see him in eyes and when their gaze meets she smiles, "do not worry lovely", to see him in tears dropping on his cheeks.

Yami pulls the rope while he is attempting to resist and makes muffled sounds. Her body half his height and weight has strength to pull him up above floor level and she ties the rope to the sidebar, leaving him above the floor.

Yami licks his ear and whispers in his ear, "do not worry mister simpleton", brushes her fingers on his neck, "I only willing to love you, remember?", slides below him and pushes his head to gaze between her legs when she picks up razor and cuts his throat open for his blood to drip over her legs.

Yami continues after every kiss to cut around his body, making her become excited and more messaging her fingers into his body. Her face miles, "I want it all", and she slices off one of his testicles to lick her finger with it.

His face in torment makes her continue to smile and she slides her legs open in front of him, while their gaze is together and he has now no more tears in his eyes, she is pulling a nail hammer her sister left her tonight to help have a good bath. Winking her fingers, "bye bye", she starts without stopping, smashing the hammer into his head over his face, when she believed she delivered the final blow she did not stop because knew it was his nerves twitching while she was having her joy.

Her relief to finish him with a good workout made her feel like getting up for a stretch.

She kicked him aside making a way to a rope with his useless head to allow her to reach the knot, "how man can be useless", her pulling rope was making him go further to the ceiling.

The shower was having more hot steam than before when she heard her signal of classical symphony number 5. It was her sister's signal to start her blood bath.

Yami took a grey -colored wooden handle sushi knife, made of fine black Japanese steel you can buy in majority shops in the capital here.

The step back in a hot shower made her soft butt cheek sit; her hands cut his guts open to let his blood and organs mixing with the heat and water fall on her head, reminding her of early spring rain.

The joy of rubbing his insides with blood over her body was worth his life.

Later on, Yami throws her sister's towel back at her, "it was worthwhile the trip." Nami looks at her and smiles, "have you flushed the dirt?", Yami takes a seat on grey sofa and opens a bottle of water, "yes, I cut him to 356 pieces and washed it the drain, but you know how I say if you smile after the dinner.", Nami is laughing, "They will take your teeth out? Oh, and I thought we attended the same assassination school.", Yami makes no comments and closes her eyes for the moment.

***

Into the dark night a campfire is making sparking sounds of fire wood burning and three friends are sitting together on a large piece of driftwood.

Simon takes one piece of sausage and stabs it on a tree branch before placing it on fire, "Did you know that Japanese Shamanism loves to soak the bloodbath of their victims they take to mark Amaterasu?

Ignacius turns to Simon, "Do not tell me shat stories by the fire in the middle of a dark forest at night. I already have bad dreams.", he stabs one sausage too and points it in fire.

Mage smiles, "buuuuuuUUUuuu", then looks in a bag for sausage too.

Ignacius, "Ignacius by the way, who the hell is Ameterasu?", he turns his sausage on the campfire to fry it even.

Simon, "She is a goddess of fire."

Ignacius, "Yeah, right. It is like our pagan god of Thunder with his symbol of Oak the tree even thunder cannot break."

Soft sounds of wind brushing against the leaves of forest trees and dead silence besides a couple of Ovals making sounds, the abandoned campsite is a good place to soak in the forest. Prison van is just making a slight noise with the prison guard making sounds of struggle to set himself free from ropes Ignacius has tied to him.

The rest fugitives are in a wooden cabin since their first day out of prison and their first night in a decent bed. They are not even concerned about having their dinner fast asleep.

Crimson Island

Early in the morning Ignacius wakes up other two fugitives to ask them if they agree to train for an important mission for their freedom.

Their names were Bob Jumbo and Dylan Mambo and were eager to start their firearms training with Simon.

The same day Bob told Simon he knows well about masochist FE Blond fashion for fetishism and about eminent torture chambers he likes to get his way.

Later in the day, the training starts and Lord Ignacius takes a cup of fresh water, "Now I miss well our Reno Marihuana from Crimson Prison"

Simon, "I hear they made it well."

They start basic tactical combat training while moving across forest with the raised hand of Simon to the direction every second points their stick to a different side; with another hand gesture they take an aim on one knee.

Mage is observing them from above on the tree branch, having his sandwich and small bottle of water for his lunchtime.

They take lunch break too and Mage points them out on their timing and space control mistakes while they do point of contact training.

Bob Jumbo, "We are like Robin Hood and the boys now taking back from the Sheriff."

Ignacius, "We are little far from them since we do not have any money."

Simon, "how our dear Detective Simpleton is getting on without us."

Ignacius, "he is like a psycho. Do you remember him talking about four archangels, justice, and the rest of weird stuff."

Simon, "how he is planning and why our Vice-Commander draw urgent request to assist him with this mission."

Ignacius, "Yeh we are on a mission impossible déjà vuuuu."

Simon, "I see Crimson werewolf awuuu."

Ignacius, "While coopers of Gothminster arresting a werewolf of capital awwuuuu out of their vans," they all laugh at a good joke.

***

Then later on the day Detective Simpleton was sitting at home and staring in his old painting made from white and black paint.

He never could understand why inherited this painting but he admires day break shadows covering their oil point adding more texture in his living room when Archangel dissents from the sky.

The Archangel closes its black wings and kneels before him, "We have another message for you about apocalyptical justice", Mr Simpleton places his cup of tea and swallows the remaining drop of tea in his mouth.

Simpleton makes a religious gesture and speaks to one of Archangels, "I was fine four weeks ago running my independent agency but four of you guys had to wake me up in a middle of the night about pending disaster and now I have to run errands for you guys like a madman around here."

Archangel with a deep voice announces the message for our Detective Simpleton, "You should know the skies above are pleased you assist us and would like to let you know you must head two o'clock outside Gothminster House of Lords to serve the justice to be continued."

Simpleton takes his check coat and pair of his glasses, "You guys cannot be told difference by looks nor by sound of voice, and always points me in a direction with another mosaic before I leave."

Archangel claps its large wings and before it leaves he says, "Much appreciated from skies above".

Our Detective heads off when he purchases a ticket on a tram and joins aboard to the direction of the Houses of Gothminster stop; while a missing prison transport is heading to the same direction.

The prison transport turns into a straight lane leading straight to House of Gothminster, speeding over speed limit over passing other vehicles like a standstill when they crash through personnel gates in order to the gardens of Crimson Ministry.

They jump out of a blue and white van saying 'Crimson Correctional Transport', and pull out extended cartridge assault rifles, opening live ammunition fire how they did training in the woods. When Dylan cannot open the closed lock, Simon says, "You beat it", when he knocks the door handle down with a firearm handle and kicks the doors open.

The team moves in a straight line holding their firearms over each other's shoulders opening rounds of fire at any member of personnel they can see in their vision.

When the team approaches the stairs, the guards of the House are rushing to the lower floor. Ignacius orders to surround the staircase for tactical ambush and Simons shouts when the House Guards approach their vision, "Attack in Attack!", then they open fire looking through gun triggers aiming every dropped round for contact with headshot.

They move upstairs taking careful steps, bending their knees and pushing with their feet the bodies of dead security personnel, with Mage behind them navigating the tourist map.

Simon, "I am happy today was closed to tourists for renovation needs", Mage continues to browse through the map for the fastest route to the Head of Ministry chambers.

They reach the chambers after quick rounds of fire when they kick the doors open to see the office abandoned in a rush, then Mage radios through a signal, "Bob if you with us you should be able to see outside Prison van a black escort leaving in about five, you can open live round on second transport".

The hand radio is cracking and he can hear Bob's voice, "I thought you guys already forgot about me, I was not even sure these building site walkies-talkies will work.", he pauses for a minute then he continues, "I can see them". The tactical team now in upstairs chambers can hear the sudden gun fire down below when Mage shows a hand signal to leave from Gothminster House.

Yet Simon smashes the office window and opens fire on a second vehicle with a Car15 assault rifle at the vehicle on an escape route, "I am sure our Bob cannot count and I added some ammunition to help our boy". When Simon stops, they make a run down the stairs back through staff rooms towards the van; along the way, Ignacius is counting the dead bodies they left behind in today's countermeasure mission.

They run past a van for Bob to join them together and when they reach the river near House of Gothminster; they take a Police speed boat for their escape transport.

***

The moments before attack FE Blond VE May was having a cup of tea in their chambers boardroom, "It is a sad moment to learn our E David had passed away, we are not sure how to let the nation know about our loss yet", when VE May blinks her eyes and takes her look away from FE Blond, "who is in charge now when your dirty ass gets whipped all the time around when we come to this".

A Terrorist attack interrupted their alarm and left for Gothminster Library's secret passage in the underground car park to board secure vehicles taking them to the Safe House briefing.

VE May fastens her seat belt, "I hate these fools causing havoc around our home", when sudden shots fire from above hits her twice in abdominal and one direct hit in her skull leaving out her jaw, FE Blond takes cover one her lap after he get shot in his shoulder and secure escort non stop drives off to Safe House.

While FE blond is laying on dead body lap and is attempting to regain his mind, he is thinking to himself why he had to agree to put in place his E David unapproved drug trial allowing women medicine causing birth defects; it was his last thoughts before he woke up in Military Security Hospital.

***

When Detective Simpleton made it in time to reach the House of Gothminster, he could see his teammates and other two men making their great escape. He understood they would need his help, and he came home to take his weekend car.

They made it in the 1980s and is wide built, allowing many passengers in sedan versions but due to fuel consumption he did not use it.

He drives along the river to spot similar looking individuals and park right before them along the street, "I am afraid it is only deluxe vehicle service today operating", for them to smile and to board vintage cars.

They make a round turn and drive until they reach the red light. But while still at traffic lights, two police officers approached them on a foot patrol.

The female officer knocks on a passenger window and Dylan lowers the car window door down holding a handgun under his jacket pointing at her through the passenger door.

She smiles and lowers her head to the passenger door, bending her back to her male colleague, "I love your car and could see you took a U-turn in single lane traffic".

Simpleton smiles and makes an apology about a minor traffic violation promising to avoid his mistake, "I am so sorry I was in a hurry to drop off my nephews to football practice, and now I can hear this commotion around.

I was in a hurry to avoid traffic", female officer smiles, "Because I love your car and we are little in a hurry I let you go without a ticket", she turns her eyes up like she would think twice, "But I would love to have your number my dear", and she blinks before she turns around and walks away.

Gothminster

L

et's continue following our young guns travelling in the belly of the beast while leaving police lines to not cross in every hot corner.

Meanwhile, in the train station a foreign woman is assaulted on the platform when men are screaming at her while they are attacking her, "Go back home where you come from, you biatch", they are kicking her on the floor while she is helpless gasping for air asking for help.

A week later the region council office worker is passing by with his proud pin badge written on it he is To Be Proud Dark Lord Servant but he does not know he is followed behind by a group of young men, they targeted him down the street when they observed his blue suit.

One of the young men approaches him and asks him if he has a lighter, the Council Officer worker responds he does not smoke and he rather prefers him to walk away.

But the remaining group of young men runs up behind him and places a dirty bin bag over his face. They just took the bag off the nearby bin.

The first young man he approached punches him in a solar plexus, making him lose air and grip on his feet. Then he kicks the officer worker in his head while he is losing his consciousness on his knees and the remaining group kicks him on the floor.

The young man takes a lighter out of his pocket and places his backpack on the floor next to him, "a shame they taught you rubbish in law school."

He opens his backpack and takes out 3 liters cider bottle full of petrol; he pours the petrol over Council Officer workers' body and lights him on fire for him to wake up in agony of fire all over his body; he tries to stand up taking off the bin bag off his face and run but he trips over the platform and is killed by expressway train, making his body torn to many parts.

The young man places his lighter in his pocket and taps his friends over their shoulders, "very great work lads when we serve our community just right", they all walk away laughing.

****

The same day when the incident took place in the capital's outskirts train station, not far away in Crimson Island, the army hospital is recovering FE Blond. He opens his eyes and can see a nurse near him; he taps his palm on her bottom while she is taking a reading from the life support monitor and orders her to bring in a doctor in charge of his care.

While he smiles he says to himself, "I am lucky now the entire country is in my hands."

When she comes back with his doctor, FE Blond learns he was lucky to escape a fatal wound because the firearm bullet went through his arm clean but the doctor announced his female colleague was fatally wounded.

FE Blond sits with the help of his nurse and tastes his cup of tea, "I am sad about such horrors we experienced as a country, I must request an immediate visit from police and army chiefs to see me, due to the sad deaths of my superiors I am now the leader of Crimson Nation."

While the military hospital was arranging an emergency summit not far away, three friends were camping and cooling down their feet in cold water.

Simon, "I wonder how long we need to stay low in our campsite before the next expedition to resume the order our Simpleton has drafted us for?"

Mage, "I am not sure because I cannot contact our HQ since we made an entry."

Ignacius, "so strange we have gone through so much but not much avail to stop the evil deeds."

Simpleton walks up to them on lake pier and asks them to follow him to the cabin where Dylan and Bob are waiting to further plan how to restore order for them to complete their mission.

While on the other side of the capital Yami and Nami are walking to their prearranged date with the lovely police officer, they find him on a local dating application on their mobile.

Yami, "I wonder what kind of candy is our mister police officer."

Nami, "I am sure he is sweet as a candy in our mouth", then she licks her lips and both girls laugh.

They come near the station of the wild nature park and are waiting outside the bus stop where the police officer promised blind double date.

The black limousine stops near them and the passenger seat window pulls down for them to learn their double date inside their car.

The men were joking when driving to the natural reserve site about their date and how they will get quick sex in back of their car and they later toss these stupid girls far away, making them walk back all the way they came.

Then when the car window pulls down Nami waves a brown hair man, and Yami blinks her left eye before they board the government issued transport.

They drive a single kilometer further to the car park before they park in an unused road under construction, Nami switches seats with the driver to sit closer with the police chief and his driver takes the back seat closer to Yami.

Nami smiles and brushes his suit and tie rubbing his left leg closer to his groin but she pulls tight a knot of his tie twisting his gaze to the passenger seat for spills of blood drop on his face.

The blood is coming from his driver's mouth while all arteries on his neck and blood vessels on his face are turning black and Yami is holding his driver by his throat.

Yami pulls a tie towards her and turns the Police Chief gaze to her, "That snot nose thought he would blaze in our stomach. But how about you?"

She pulls out her lollipop, pops out her mouth with her left arm from his hip and stabs him two times in his groin.

She pulls his tie over her shoulder, meeting their shoulder together in a hug, she places her mouth closer to his ear, "Shhh do not worry".

Then she rubs her arm from his groin to his stomach up and down, for the poison to flow quicker. He dies in her arms.

When Yami and Nami finish pulling dead bodies in the trunk of their car, Yami checks their wallets, "Great, we just finished the Police Chief and his driver."

Nami smiles and kicks their legs in to close the trunk, "we inherited their wheels on our first date".

She shouts out of happiness and jumps up clapping her hands in the air, "we will now not need to walk around now".

Yami, "Great, I am already tired."

The poison was from black crab, the nerves paralysis poison only found in their native home shores.

They dip the needles in a pure extract of black crab venom and concealed them inside sticks of sweets they packed inside their bag before their flight.

The poison is the strongest in the entire world, making a man's heart stop in three seconds from nerve paralysis, and since so effective no one ever had an idea to create an antidote for the venom.

While the girls boarded their borrowed government vehicle and were placing their make-up looking at the rear mirrors of their vehicle, on the other side of the triangle of location point; Simon was opening a tin of black shoe wax.

He dips his two fingers inside the tin and is making straight line marks on his face, then brushes wax off with a wet towel and places another direction of shoe wax once more.

Mage walks in to see Simon using shoe wax, "ok to adjust war paint to your face contours but do not forget we will end up without if you use it all."

Simon turns around, "Do not worry, I am almost done."

Mage looks at him from the chair. He places his feet on the table and inspects Simon's face, "Well done, you look great."

Simon Says, "Let's show them northern European mind games."

Mage, "Well better than Ignacius painting black only his eyes and his lips."

**

Two weeks after the disappearance of the Police Chief with his driver and FE Blond resuming powers of his nation, now he is Excellency Blond and is making an appearance with his financial donors in a government owned golf course.

Sinbury

hen Simon approaches His Excellency golf course, he shows them the Art of War and takes the Excellency in for questioning about his intentions to the Nation.

Ignacius is walking next to Simon. He has cast clay arm over his left arm with bandage over it to keep it straight over his shoulder.

Ignacius, "The bottles you", before Simon looks around how to infiltrate pass security and exit routes to have Blond handed back in their camp.

Simon walks past the alleyway and picks up an empty bottle of wine. He relaxes his shoulders and sways his arms to sides when he walks up to security guards.

He walks up a meter apart from the guard at the side entrance and sways over the head of security guards to see how the second security officer reaches for his hand radio with the intention to press the panic button.

Ignacius spends no time waiting and hits the guard over his face with a cast clay arm, he rushes in his right arm in a cast clay arm and slashes over the neck of the security officer. Ignacius is standing there and is catching his breath with a long slim blade in his hand. The blood splatters from the cut are just leaking off the wooden doors.

The entrance is not a common type to enter the golf field; it is at the end of a small alleyway, made of a stone wall covered in moss and reaffirmed by a steel, wooden door.

Simon takes out two rain jackets from his backpack and handles one to Ignacius.

Ignacius, "I now cursed us dagger daggering Crimsoners?"

Simon inspects Ignacius' right hand, "I think you would fit the description far better than me".

Simon places his bottle in a backpack and takes out a tin of black shoe wax.

He places two lines across his face of shoe wax.

Then he passes the shoe wax to Ignacius to see him draw black circles around his eyes and on his lips.

Simon, "We will need to keep our heads low under our coats until we reach Blond, then war paint across our faces will distort our images in their security cameras, giving better chances not to be detected."

Ignacius, "I am sure my face paint will give them creeps."

Simon, "I felt uncomfortable already."

They jump over a stone fence since they could not find the keys and continue walking along the bushes and ponds looking around for a blonde man.

His Excellency Blond at the time went inside the top floor of the golf course building to toast a glass of champagne with his financial donors. He was talking about the next election strategy and his great past success, making him leader of Crimson Nation.

His speech did not go ahead so well as he planned because Simon and Ignacius were looking through glass doors in the balcony to make sure it was him who would be taken together with them to their campsite.

Simon throws in a steel chair from the balcony to allow them access to the lounge and create a diversion of confusion, the element of surprise they needed to successfully capture His Excellency.

When E Blond hears the sounds of shattering windows, he screams to sound the alarms and his bodyguards rush him and VIP guests to the rooftop of the building. It was all according to Blond's plan.

When he learned they nearly shot him dead from above him when he was escaping Gothminster, he ordered his security to give him other security plans rather than the last failed ones.

Simon is wasting no time and enters the scene of chaos. The staff and guests are covering their heads in a rush from sides to sides.

The moment of despair allows Simon to manipulate bodies, pushing them in the way of guards when he hits them over their heads with his wine bottle, then he reverses and smacks his elbow in the security's face.

He takes his deep breath and kicks the table over to shield his stance.

He does a 360 degree round house kick in the guard's head walking behind the table. He trips over another guard with the same table he kicked over.

Simon picks up the table by its legs because he can see most of the guests have evacuated and now is wide enough open space for them to use their firearms.

He rushes the table to the remaining security, pressing them to open the doorway.

The image is indescribable, such as a painting of war; the bodies of ten men one over another attempting to weigh down Simon just to give them their space to reach their holster.

Ignacius is wasting no time and starts running across a long table with his feet kicking aside all the drinks and meals left on the plates.

He attempts to jump over Simon, only landing a hard elbow and breaking the jaw of security. But he did not come empty-handed and stabbed him in the neck with his concealed blade.

Ignacius does not stop with a single strike of his blade and continues stabbing them across their jaws, necks, ears and eyes for Simon to realise the pressure pushing his end of the table is decreasing.

Ignacius pushes Simon aside from the table, "Let me cleanse this well."

He then continues stabbing into the table until he understands there is no more gasping, there is no more struggle on the other end of their table.

Simon quickly leans hard against the wood table side and makes a run to the top floor, looking for His Excellency.

Excellency Blond is taking a shelter under large clay flower basins with his two top donors, their names are Mr Bill and Mr Merlin. He is leaning behind the basin and is looking at how security personnel are pointing their handguns towards the doors.

He taps back on Mr Bill and nods looking at them, "Do not worry, everything will be great. I am not for no reason the number one leader of our nation."

When he can hear loud breathing behind his back and smoothing dripping on the tile floor. When he looks back, it is too late because Ignacius was standing right behind him.

His Excellency screams only to learn Ignacius pulls him back, taking him for a live shield and having a sharp blade covered in blood pointing across his neck.

When security understands the gravity, they are standing and turning their handguns around.

Simon kicks the door open pushing one guard over the floor and before the second guard makes his way back pointing his gun to Simon, he hits him over his head with a bottle of wine.

While he dazed the guard from the blow to his skull, Simon takes his right arm pointing towards the floor and squeezes his finger to fire a shot to the chest.

The direct shot penetrates one security officer's chest, but Simon takes no chances and presses his foot on the firearm that is left on the floor.

He three seconds later kicks aside the gun he was holding under his foot, and twists the hand of the officer's hand he is holding.

They walk and from the twist from his neck to his right arm finger tips pain is unbearable causing him to drop his gun.

Simon continues walking towards kicking his knees down the legs of the security guard, walking past Ignacius and throws the guard off the balcony.

Mr Bill and Mr Merlin looked below them from the balcony to see what they left of security to keep them safe.

When he was falling down he hit his skull hard enough on the side of the building to reveal the insides of his head, then he fell on an enormous gap between the pool floor and steps to tables.

His legs were turned left and his neck was so stretched on the sidewalk it was obvious enough it got detached from the spine.

When Ignacius orders Blond to move and keep his mouth shut, Mr Bill grabs a brick from the side of a large clay basin and aims for his head.

But Simon kicks him aside, making a path for Ignacius to continue escorting their hostage..

He takes no further chances and grabs Bill on the side of his neck and pushes him through a glass rail to meet the same fate they had just witnessed.

Simon took a quick look below him to understand the same brick had in his hand now was in Merlin's hand aiming back of his head.

He ducked the blow to the back of his skull and kicked Merlin's feet, making him lose his balance. While Merlin was taking a second to regain his balance, Simon pulled his arm towards the glass railing and pushed his neck in shards of broken glass.

Simon kicked Merlin's neck deeper in broken glass, leaving his dying eyes looking down below him.

Ignacius was standing to doorway to stairs and was punching Blond in his stomach, "Simon, hurry, I know shat happens but if we do not hurry, we will cover more casualties along the way!"

Simon spat down below and rushed towards Ignacius to help him secure His Excellency and head back to their campsite to start his interrogation.

Simon throws F Blond in the back of his car trunk, "You cannot do this to me, I study law university and I am a leader of this supreme nation", Simon shuts the trunk.

Ignacius, "Yeah right, he is lucky for now not to end up like Bill Twatter and Merlin D Cup", he smiles when they walk to board Blond's escort vehicle.

Simon, "I study life's university."

Ignacius before takes a passenger seat, slaps the trunk a couple times and says, "Good luck, my friend."

The Sinbury, Boys!

Threenight before our heroes are interrogating His Excellency Blond Da Dirta Cossack, somewhere on the motorway is speeding a thunder truck with a sticker written on it: Power-Up.

Simon the night before was dreaming about a giant cat burning the world with a strike of match and he is afraid every night the nightmares will continue.

But now they throw Blond on the floor in a campsite cabin for Bob and Dylan to kick him on the floor, the kicks are turning so violent Blond is thinking his guts will burst open his sides are stinging so much. But Bob and Dylan are not thinking to stop warming him until they acknowledge a puddle of blood coming out from their enemy.

Mage walks in and places his mug of coffee before he tells them to stop beating him and take him to the lake pier for fresh midnight water. "I prefer him to have a good wash to see his face telling the truth before us rather than him dead in a pile of his own shat in our cabin."

They pull Blond on his legs outside the cabin towards the lake, spitting on him along the way because he is moaning about the injuries he sustained at the start of their inquiry to his plans.

He opens his swollen eyes up when they take a bin bag off his head and he can see the stars from above the night sky. He can feel his arms and legs tied up to a metal chair.

His body temperature is far greater at the moment than the rusty metal chair they trapped him in, and he does not feel at ease.

Mage slaps him across his face two times, feeling the blood on his hand from his bleeding face.

"I hope you rather stop stargazing tonight or I murder you on the spot before you spill the beans of your evil deeds."

"I swear it was the Dark Lord and his Evil Viking Princess.

They contemplated selling unapproved medicines to pregnant women causing birth defects and the former Excellency of Crimson Nation, our David, covered the case up by sending the victims to a madhouse."

"I assume you were an underdog assuming nothing about it and only pushing the pencils to make your career goals go further?"

"I swear it was not me, I only did what I was told."

But Simon smiles and walks one step closer. He steps over a metal chair and smacks his boot in Blond's neck.

"I am sure you are no good fool, same as your forefathers, to be proud satanic island nation supreme commanders who started two global wars and massacred many nations of people leaving piles of corpses behind them."

Then he watches how E Blond is gasping for air from his wide open throat. He turns around holding his heel on his crushed throat and feels how his stomach is growling inside him.

"Because your ancestors displaced the entire planet's population in poverty and death so you could be proud at least I can feel your mouth with my warm shat, matey." He lets his belt slip and drops his butt cheeks on Blond.

He felt a relief only for a moment Simon's foot came off his dry throat but now he can't breathe much longer feeling feces floating down his mouth, overflowing from sides of his mouth causing him gasping chokes on his throat.

Simon stands up and watches how the wild eyes of His Excellency Blond have lost its focus. His throat is throwing hick-ups, flowing feces and his stomach content out of his mouth for another try to live one. "I am sorry mates, I could not hold myself together allowing him to set free, I wanted to know he had good feed at yesterday's banquet."

Magnum Mage walks over his stomach heading back to the cabins and while he is walking away, he asks his mates to dip into the water with their Excellency Blond for a good wash before they load him up back into their truck.

They tie the knot of the rope to their chain and Ignacius kicks a metal chair over into the lake to pull back up afloat and merge him under the water. "This shat bag is hell heavy."

***

Our Bob Mumbo and Dylan Jumbo were Crimson Nation Sumo Federation leaders, and had the nickname Demolition Brothers for their own reason.

Mage was driving their black truck and was learning further about their destined new teammates. He was picked up from Crimson Prison.

They learned through Detective Simpleton the mental health hospital in Sinbury is keeping victims of illegal drugs from Dark Lord imprisoned under false claims they were insane.

They pull to third gear and drove Capital Road A30 leading to Sinbury to meet their future perspectives Detective Simpleton recommended for his biblical justice prevail.

***

Simon was already in Sinbury before the rest of the heroes arrived at the location Simpleton told to operate a commando mission and walked into a local firearms store.

"I wonder how many crowns it would be for this pellet rifle on display." He points his finger at camouflage model 300X, with a high velocity sniper frame gun with a sticker on it stating it was great for scaring crows of your trees.

The gun store keeper passes a pellet rifle to Simon and lets him know today they are having 10% sale if he purchases it with a 2000 pallet package.

"What a focking sale mate!" He smacks the store keeper in the face with the other end of his rifle and jumps over the counter, hitting him over the head.

"It is a focking sale matey." He continues beating the gun seller, hitting his skull with his thick boots.

He then walks up to the store front and flips the sign over to the store that is closed and closes the lock behind him.

"As we say where I am from, I was not born on a bus." He walks up to the unconscious but still breathing gun store keeper and takes him back to the storage room to find these 2000 pallets he promised him 10% discount.

Simon walks out back of the store and looks up to the sunny skies above Sinbury, aims and fires at the town square circle made out steps made to sit and have lunch for local office workers.

He licks his finger to see the wind direction and counts his breath by the wind speed, observing local wind breeze coming through two to three-storey buildings round the main town square.

"Business as usual."

When he is 30 meters away from town square, a car park is on the second floor above the supermarket.

He takes a short walk thinking the perfect wind direction will help him fire and aim at the Crimsoners at town Square.

He takes two streets left, believing he will make it in time to reach his spot to open fire, but he notices a man standing at a cash machine near the car park.

The man is looking right at him, observing Simon. He sights, "I think I start sooner rather than later." Simon waves at a man crossing his path, "Hey old man!"

He throws his rifle forward, "Catch it mate." Simon rushes up to him while the rifle lands in man's hands. He kicks his boot tip in his groin and snatches his rifle back from his hands.

Simon hits him over his face with his rifle. He takes a step aside and hits his happy customer two times in the neck, smashing his head further in a cash machine cracking its screen.

"I am sure that one will be attempted robbery.", when he walks away from his first happy customer.

He walks up the stairs and then he aims and fires with every breath he takes.

Shooting one office worker's ear off, he hits one in his hand and fires a third shot in his ass while there is panic in the town square between officer workers scattering them and running with panic.

Simon takes a seat and opens a can of soda water to see how fast they will find in the car park but before he finishes his drink the firearms officers locate and surround him, "Hands on your head and drop to the floor!"

He takes advice from firearms officers and kneels down the floor holding his hands above him.

When he walks up before the judge, crown prosecution announces charges and brief history of his case, "This man is a wanted fugitive, our dear justice, he committed homicide and assisted in another homicide with another fugitive in the wanted criminals list."

Simon's lawyer takes defence and asks him to be detained before we will hold further medical advice upon crown courthouse.

He then asks Simon to take a stand in the witness box to speak his statement in order for the judge to process his case.

Simon walks the aisle with heavy steel cuffs on his both hands and feet, he steps in a witness box and scratches his forehead, "I only wished to make my customers happy, I was working so long keeping shoes clean my dear liege, and I aimed hard to keep it this way."

The judge looks to the defence lawyer and asks him to explain the speech the defendant had just said, "I hope I satisfied you or would like to hear the defendant's further thoughts on his statement."

But before the judge places his hammer, "I am from Ruso planet and I love outstanding women like your daughter, mister judge."

Then the judge shouts it is enough of this and orders him to keep two weeks in high restriction local asylum to see how he will respond to treatment before he can make further decisions.

Sinbury at Midnight

T

hey summoned Simon up to the crown's courthouse, and Ignacius was holding plans for the battle of his own.

He was sitting and thinking how Mage is doing with Bob and Dylan to dump His Excellency's body to northern marshes to make him walk back all his way back to Crimson Capital.

The sun was strong, and he was feeling the warmth in his body on the beach near Sinbury. He would rather turn around on his back and have more sunshine before he takes his part in a commando mission.

The Curse Dagger operation in his mind was too much to handle, but he knew it would determine the fate of the satanic island nation.

His wrist watch alarm beeped twice, and he had to be up from comfortable dunes of sand. He hoped on his bike that within 45 minutes of cycling he would reach the destination.

Sinbury was a low profile rural town, but after Simon's attack it was so silent it felt to Ignacius, he could slice such thick silence with his knife.

While picking up speed on the bicycle lane, Ignacius pulls out behind his leather belt a sharp sushi knife he bought in Crimson Capital.

Ahead of him was cycling to medical emergency response cyclists because of the heat wave that day on patrol in case of heat stroke.

"Screw you perverts!" Ignacius shouts and slashes, passing by one of the first responders' neck while the second is attempting to provide first aid. Ignacius stabs him, piercing the tip of his blade through the chest.

"I knew this would make a scene on camera.", speaks under his breath and starts cycling away.

He was right and security cameras captured the incident and filmed a clear picture of Ignacius' face.

It took not long before police officers apprehended Ignacius when he made couple cuts through their vests.

Our Ignacius in the courthouse case has pleased prosecution to provide another suspect of murder.

Their officers captured the fugitive on the run.

"I am an actor and I was filming pornography scenes. I plea not guilty and I shall sleep with your wife if you wish me so, dear court liege!"

But the judge had no excuses and ordered pretrial for mental health tribunal hearing after two weeks investigation in a top security unit.

***

The same night when two patients were administered to a mental health hospital, they found His Excellency Blond naked wandering in the woods and summoned to explain himself to his Dark Lord.

He walks in the chambers of Dark Castle and kneels on his knees before his liege to say, "I regret my failures, your majesty."

The Dark Lord is having a glass of fine wine and on his knees is sitting his blonde mistress. He orders his women to step aside while he inspects in the eyes of this fool.

He stands up and slaps the bottom of his mistress, "My dear Viking Princess, let me set this straight or we will have less time to bathe."

Then walks up to Blond and picks him up on his jaw to smack him hard in his face, but mister Blond thinks to himself it was not as painful as how these fugitives kicked his guts.

"Do you understand why we keep you alive!"

"We need you to cover up after us, like a singer in our toilet singing for us while we feel a need to have a dump on his face!"

"You complete fool, clowns can do better than you to make me angry!"

Dark Lord smacks Blond in his stomach and drops him on the floor.

"I would shag Vikings Princess, you watching us, but I am afraid I would strangle you after, you incompetent fool!"

Meanwhile, the Dark Lord leads his Viking Princess to natural roman baths to have a night filled with pleasure. On the other side of the Nation, Yami and Nami are making a prayer.

Yami and Nami kneel before a large stone, and light their match to set a small fire out of driftwood as they gather inside the Dark Woods Forest.

"You think it will keep their bodies warm."

Nami inspects the distance between two dead bodies they hang upside above their stone altar and fire set above a large stone.

"I am sure it will be enough distance to stop them setting on fire."

"The stars are so bright tonight, it is the perfect shape to complete our ritual for Bakura."

The Bakura, Yami was referring to as their God of Necessary Evil they must offer dead bodies of victims they killed before the gods from above shall approve their wishes come true.

"I think it is enough", Yami says, and lights a torch. She pushes burning wood off the stone and stamps on it with foot to stop fire spreading further and places matcha tea bowl under their dead bodies.

Nami takes a step closer and stabs dead men in their necks, allowing their blood to drip in a large tea bowl underneath them. They both smile, share a round cup of black blood and kiss each other on the lips.

"I think the last part was unnecessary", and they both start laughing after their Pagan God ritual is complete.

***

The time twin sisters finished their ritual, Simon was trying to close his eyes in the government hospital bed. He felt so uncomfortable he could not close his eyes in this ward. The place seemed wrong, and he could not understand it yet.

One of the ward nurses on patrol was completing his rounds of checks before he signed off on his duty. He was taking a step closer to a room Simon was in.

He opened the door hatch and turned the light on to inspect how the new patient was doing.

"Mate, are you ok, I hope you feel comfortable here."

"Hey mate, speak up!"

He takes out his key and opens the door to Simon's bedroom. He walks closer to his bed, not taking his eyes away from the duvet he is covered up in.

His hand is sliding to his pocket, and he is taking out a syringe of venom the Dark Lord Castle's servant gave him before his day on duty, with instructions to stab Simon in his neck.

One meter apart from him and Simon, he jumps on top of his bed and stabs through the duvet in the syringe, letting the venom out.

But Simon was no fool that night and he doubled up his duvet to hide himself aside from the edge of his bed.

Simon kicks the nurse off his bed and stops him breathing, suffocating him with a knee on his windpipe. Simon stands up and takes the keys of the dead body.

"I am sure I could use a tour before my team arrives."

He walks down the corridor at night to open the fire exit door and walks two floors below to the women's ward to see a picture in horror.

Three men are making fun out of their patient. They have her on the pool table, both legs apart.

Two are holding her both arms apart while the other is sticking his insides in-between her legs.

"I can see you are saying you are not insane. Try saying this to your doctor", he says, while he is laughing together with his fellow nurses and pushing deeper and harder inside her.

Simon takes a moment to look and starts walking towards them along the way, taking with him a pool table bat.

He walks up behind the nurse with his pants down and stabs him in butt.

The half-naked nurse is screaming in agony and pushes away from his patient.

But he does not stop and grabs him around his neck with his bat.

"You should lick it clean when ya fock up matey", Simon says, and he pushes the nurse's face between her legs the same moment breaking his neck on the pool table.

Two other nurses let go of the patient's hands and started walking toward Simon. He hits one nurse over his face and breaks his bat and hits the third villain approaching him.

The group of nurses rushes out the emergency exit door and Simon throws his half broken bat across the hall to stab the first nurse in her eye to the doors of the emergency exit.

But to Simon's demise the poor girl who abused picked up a pool ball and hit his head behind him over five times to make him pass away.

The moment he died the clocks stopped and black smoke started coming out behind hall doors. Nurses ignored the surrounding moment while they were attempting to restrain the poor victim of violence.

"You all are fools and rapists", she was screaming her lungs out. But the moment a black figure appeared opposite her in full steel armour, she froze in fear.

The figure thought to himself, in what time and era I wonder in my sleeps on stones of time he traveled.

"Who dares to call his majesty of Grand Duchy", when he says, all the nurses stop restraining the patient and turn back frozen in fear.

He looks at them and with a gesture on the palm of his hand they kneel before him, unable to bear the weight of their bodies on the floor. He continues watching them in silence.

"What a focking freak are now on loose?" One nurse pushes his words out of his throat.

"I can sense the sex magic of these fools", the Grand Duke says to himself and the Pagan Lord necromancer, with the swing of his finger to side, wakes up Simon from dead.

He then points his finger to the nurses and Simon attacks them, massacring them to pieces, ripping with his abnormal human strength apart their organs in his blood thirst.

Simon can see himself from inside him but he cannot gather the moment he feels weak and now sees his body moving on its own, killing with supreme strength those nurses and the patient too many bits.

"Now sleep my son, I blessed you with the sign of Grand Duke's crest", when the ancient Lord Necromancer relaxes his hand Simon falls deep into sleep.

When he wakes up in the morning in a padded cell, he cannot place pieces of puzzle together from a new dream he had.

Sinbury Screams!

The knock wakes up Simon in his blue padded cell. His head is feeling from last night and the dream he had was nothing usual, at least he thought.

The cell hatch opens up and the ward nurse announces the ward doctor is ready to see him for a ward round. The nurse says, "If you are feeling stable and sound for our visit let us know."

Simon turns around under the blanket and nods his head. His eyes are feeling drowsy, he can open the lids of his eyes to see them.

The doctor walks in the blue room after nurses secure the safe space to talk with their patient Simon. Doctor says, "I heard you last night had some trouble sleeping and caused an emergency state in our facility."

"It was black magic."

"I am sure it was. I would like to know more about it.", says the doctor, nodding his head to the nurse taking her notes. But Simon refuses to talk more and closes his eyes. He faces the other side of the room and falls fast asleep.

Meanwhile, our friend Ignacius is just settling down and not wanting to lose time is gathering information from the mental health ward he is located just a floor above Simon is captive.

He asks many questions but cannot establish any truth further from irrational talks he is having with his fellow captives in Sinbury Hospital.

Until he meets Marciuszawa, the student who is for violent behaviour for breaking several laws including anti-social behaviour, body harm and resisting arrest.

He was breaking conditions of bail. The courthouse held him to establish why he was keen enough not to comply and was on a law-breaking spree, increasing his chance to be detained further.

They found common ground after a couple cups of tea and a packet of cigarettes they smoked on the ward balcony. He understood it was taboo for male patients to learn what was in the female ward, causing more causes for concerns.

***

It took a couple days after they parked the thunder truck in a hangar outside Sinbury plains for Mage to establish local support to rescue his fellow teammates from being held captive under courthouse order.

Detective Simpleton pointed him to look for student Daku Stix in the local bar. He felt like in a pub crawl, but when he was about to give up with Bob and Dylan, the luck had made its way.

Daku Stix was philosophy faculty student, spending most of his evenings in union bars before heading out to illegal students' garage fights to earn his title after graduation as King of Hades, in Greek mythology known as underworld for dead.

He and his fellow students were now in the second year of their degree exchanging fists with their fierce rivals from law faculty. But he was having problems because they detained one of his fellows in Sinbury Asylum, and he was eager enough to set him free.

Mage walks in and sits down at the bar. He asks for a double shot of whiskey with no ice. The barman pours a glass and passes to Mage, he twists whiskey glass and pours some in his throat.

"I heard you are in your second year, Stix. I think we have some common ground here to talk business."

"I think you should go where you came from", said Stix.

"I know Marciuszawa's story and who is behind it but I am happy enough to aid you in breaking him out of that shat hole they call Hospital."

Stix orders his fellow students to sit back. He then offers a drink to Mage and asks him to step outside alone to smoke a cigarette with him in case they forge common ground.

***

The nights were getting worse for Simon after he witnessed his own death, and how he came back to life was haunting him the last three nights. He paid little attention to the screams coming from other wards but something occupied enough of him in his mind, what happened to his body he could escape death.

When he can hear along the wind a soft whistling sound coming outside his window. He can recognize the person.

Then Simon took a glimpse at moving shadows along the fence and could recognize Simon with his crew from prison, he was sure they had extra few more bodies moving along them.

When in front of the main entrance two drunk students stumble on the front steps and start urinating on main entrance doors crossing their urine streams together, one saying, "We made an X mark on the devil's gatehouse?"

It took not long before security responded through the doors asking them to leave or they would inform the police about them.

Stix gives a sly smile out of the corner of his lips and says to his fellow student he should not cross his path with this Cerberus.

"Izanagi, have you lost your mind bringing me to the gatehouse of Cerberus?"

He then punches his fellow student to the floor and then punches security guards too back to the walls, kicking and punching them splatters of blood from their broken bones.

Daku waves holding the keys in his hands for his new friends to come out behind the bushes.

He smiles and picks up Izanagi off the floor, dusting him off.

"I am a great actor Daku, your poor punch did me no good or you are just getting weaker after every shot of whiskey."

"I hope I forget what you said next weekend in the union bar, Izanagi."

They open the front gates and step in when Mage, with the rest of the guys, catches up to them at the main doors. Mage says, "Boys, we are making history here."

They inspect blueprints Detective Simpleton emailed them before tonight's fight and they split in a group, making their way in main stairs and fire exit stairs to block any attempt to escape.

Daku and Izanagi are leading their rescue party through main stairs to take back Marciuzawa, when Mage with his team are heading back to free Ignacius and Simon, including witnesses they find for operation the Cursed Dagger to finish.

The screams came out from the asylum but enough patients became quiet listening to their wardens screaming in agony and fear, when assailants were screaming at them giving the beating of their lifetime.

When our heroes are making their way up the floors, nurses fall through the windows dropping on fences or cars breaking their backs.

The dead bodies bleed out their mouths, dilated iris staring up above them, when their fingertips pointing up above them.

It was visible that others did not meet their painless death and were lying on the concrete floor with broken limbs and bleeding to death from brain damage before they found them in a morning shift.

While Ignacius was sharing his last smoke with Marciuzawa, they were observing the wardens heading in panic along the corridors when sirens were beeping without a break.

Then all they can hear windows smashing and Bob with Dylan walking and smiling to them, waving their hands as they were on a usual day visit to see their friends in a hospital ward.

Ignacius' mouth opens so wide and he can see behind them Magnum Magen with Simon Says walking along them and many other men dusting debris off their shoulders.

Marciuszawa screams he was right and philosophers cannot die because they are living proof.

Ignacius looks at Marciuzawa with surprise and comes to understand he was the only one making sense here, who said his friends will storm in here to have him back.

"But why did you tell me it was Hades' Kingdom? I am sure it is sort of graveyard sounding place."

"Junior student, you have much yet to learn."

Then Marciuzawa walks to his mates, giving them a big hug and starts walking away, tapping on each other's shoulders.

Ignacius looks at Mage, Simon, Bob and Dylan to ask them if they have finished the Cursed Dagger project.

"Do we have any intel yet because I am afraid I will catch cancer in my lungs if I stay a day longer in this place?"

Mage says, "We have set all the victims free and told them to wait a couple streets further away from the local park for Detective Simpleton to pick them up and hide them in our new safe house."

But Simon was feeling a withdrawal effect and still holding on his blanket over his shoulders, was thinking about Grand Duke and intention of his appearance the moment he died.

"What is next?"

Sinbury Scares

The one shall unseal under heavenly gates pass seven passages the seal to set free what they kept seeing us from unseen powers." Our Detective Simpleton wrote a text message to Mage after another vision could be seen from Archangels.

He said to research their former because pure evil of all kinds will deal in supreme matters but Mage could not understand his next mission point he received in his mobile.

"Ok guys, we have further plans and it is time to move out before we have time."

The nuclear Nottingham Power Station disaster the same day struck the news about an accident related to computer system malfunction but before it was the truth.

Time came over Dark Woods forest clouds to cover in heavy matter and Simon sneezed the evening feeling being watched.

Far away in a forest of large smog of dark fumes gathered and a shadow figure appeared in full black armour.

"I can see life and the force of negative energy in my dreams."

He gathered his right hand in a fist, concentrating on a ball of forbidden arts, concentrating the dark fume round his fist in electrifying focus.

It all turned into a large energy ball bewildering, turning against the axis of earth round his hand and when he released it in the palm of his hand, it disappeared into thin air.

The moment it went to sense the force of energy, it was intentional, too.

Meanwhile, at the Nuclear Management Office the nuclear panel safety worker was checking the late night shift and was taking notes of the check screen showing levels of radioactive energy bars in the safe zone when it came he did not expect.

"Mike, I am almost done with the shift controlling the emergency readings department, but when management will send John to cover the next 12 hours I could take time off?"

When his radio started receiving interference and signal sounds made cracking noises in his control management office appeared papers to lift off his table and a thin black ball appeared in mid air above him.

The Daily Crimsoners newspaper published a headline about unprecedented scale calamity stroke Crimson Nation.

Nottingham Power nuclear reactors melted in extreme overdrive and with radioactive conflagration caused massive explosions turning the site to ground zero, not leaving stone on stone making it a large dark hole below the ground it stood once.

The newspaper printed a suggestion Ministry for Crimson Energy Development Department assume preliminary findings of system mellification from computer systems failure to detect overheating overseeing cooling fan system one causing chain reaction in one blast devastating expansion reaching the time clouds above location.

When Simon read the news he said to himself he had enough of those bad feelings and it is time to penetrate further on his mission to eradicate evil, but he asked himself why he had to do it?

It is such a strange task from a detective who seemed not fit into any type of asylum.

He shook his head and continued his focus sitting by the table watching Mage briefing over the map in the middle of the table discussing the next expedition mission.

"Guys I hold a good idea about dealing final blows to these sick leaders."

Lord Ignacius reassured his plans can tackle the crimes of the Nation.

He suggested the following steps reaching above actions in mind of NATO's private security commanding officer's plans.

"I would like to like this Blond's ass on a pick once I finish playing with his wife's boobs."

"You are sicko Ignacius."

"No guys."

"You know what sadistic pervert he is. I gather that he loves to play with his wife his chikdren to see children."

"And?"

"I am sure our lovely officer Simon could pay a visit to his lonely wife at Tvartas way 10 to be of some help."

"No way!"

"You get to wear your uniform back."

"Ok."

There our young officer went to a plan befitting the most unimaginable ways of collecting the truth from sinister.

He knocks on Tvartas Way 10 asking for a cup of tea because he is feeling cold and lonely outside.

"Hello there. Where is your colleague, James? He is regular on duty."

"Mam I think he left on urgent duty and I am only here to complete security checks."

"Oh, come in there I will make a proper tea bag for you."

"I would love you to tea bag it". He then licks his lips and walks in to see her.

While original officers on duty are resting in peace with stab wounds in their heads.

***

Meanwhile Simon is pumping his Excellency Blond's wife on their bedroom table.

Yami and Nami Suki had completed their calling for God's Bakura ritual and to seal their final oath path to complete vowing of necessary evil for an unjust act.

"I am happy about it."

"You sure it will cut it?"

"Yep, it should be enough to send of evil Viking princess back home in her suitcase so they could make a statue back out of her."

"Ok but you make sure it cuts well enough, the last time I had my shoulder sore from an extra hand job."

They both laughed once Yami said it.

The time Simon gave a second shot, moaning, his ending of Kurvaa Jensen's face.

"What a strange name is Kurvaa."

"I think because it sounds nice."

"Ok Kurvaa whatever, now you lick my balls off at once."

"Oh, what a stallion you, mister officer?"

"You just call me Stanley."

He grabs her by her hair and rubs her face in it, thinking to himself she told him about her fool, everything he needs to know.

She was moaning so loud in the heart of public office with her children sleeping below.

He had his fun and left to report his finding to commanding officer Mage.

***

When Simon was back at the temporary expedition site codename 666.

She told him once he was leaving she was craving for him. Once her proud nation's leader was at home, she was far more aroused next door to him.

He reported His Excellency Blond's wife's words on the papers and took the night off early to plan tomorrow once Detective Simpleton approves planning permission.

While Yami and Nami were on their way to honour God's Bakura, wishes made at the altar avenged the innocence and fed her blood of demons.

***

Mage was in a morning navigating through plan setting the route of Vanguard to Simon, he taking the rearguard and leaving sideguard to Ignacius to oversee their rookies to freedom of our Bob and Dylan.

"It will not be as usual because our site is the walt to archives kept close to gold's deposit safe."

"It will be high guarded and armed because we are here and we killed making this Nation status to death communication 10, the top terrorism alert."

"But since we are not terrorists, we do not care. We aim and fire at them to stop pure evil from massacring the innocent world."

"Roger?"

They all screamed, "Copy That Commanding Officer Mage."

Godmorgan Era of Satan

They summoned the two hounds in Dark Castle. They wear leather and had a mission to guard his son Rudolf, the future impaler of sex, to threaten our seven heroes' futures.

While he was out to see his surroundings.

He left his castle for others to orgy he could show around his lands at night for his sex tool the Vikings had sent him. He loved his new playthings.

It chained them to the neck near toilets. The men the Dark Lord had made from honest politicians who opposed his sick laws.

He had them have sex with pigs and goats before they lost their sanity. He sexually abused their family members before they submitted themselves to pledge their loyalty for life in exchange to live another day.

Meanwhile, from outside the Dark Lord's castle, the slugs went through the young prince's chest while he was masturbating on the toilet seat.

"I think I got one prick."

"Those slugs are for those that courts won't judge, you better watch where you hit."

The demolition brothers Bob and Dylan were having a conversation behind sniper rifle optics.

Our vanguard was closing in by the castle moat to open the gates.

The time elite rearguard was watching sideguard wasting their slugs and counting ammunition to clear their path for entry to end this pure evil of Crimson Nation.

When it came in view of a depravity to vanguard enter castle's hall and see the Cabinet of Education ministers from Gothminster Palace having an orgy forcing young choir of girls from local boarding school in underage sex.

The Cabinet Ministers were forcing themselves on young girls wearing t-shirts written on them as King of Porn.

But Bob sneezes and opens fire through letter O of the cabinet minister' t-shirt, starting a scene from depravity to massacre.

"I hope this won't make trouble because the rearguard told us off already for last aimless fire."

The vanguard has nothing left but to control the situation and contribute to the first round of assault before they can let in the rearguard team waiting outside.

"I wonder what is happening from inside with all guns clapping."

"I think our guys got ambushed."

"Let's clear the bridge with grenades because we cannot confirm a positive ID."

"Sideguard, do you copy? You are open to aim and fire."

"Copy that."

When the rearguard enters the site, they flank our vanguard to a defensive corner waiting for the help because they blocked a radio signal with a transmitter blocking paint in the hall of orgy evil Dark Lord designed to keep his servants happy.

Commanding officer takes no time to open fire from his AK102 assault rifle aiming at a tactical reflective shield.

He aims below the view gap because bullets spin always upward and distance of the aim from metres determines in millimeters on his sight.

The first round goes below taking a second direct headshot at a hostile because he knows in such an exchange half a second determines if you stay alive and can carry on your assignment further.

He takes a further step to open the path for the trapped vanguard but he is held off by Dark Lord soldiers further off the hall next to colons, taking heavy fire round his shoulders in a cover.

Simon aims the feet of the last tactical shield foot soldier, making him fall down on his knees and he pushes the shield back, stepping on him to kill him through open gun fire on his face 10 centimetres apart off victims head.

When vanguard opens a clear path they move from hall to hall but are not able to find any presence of Dark Lord except the dead kid on the toilet seat before they force Simon to shoot dead two guys in dark Spandex suits with dog collars chained in front of the entrance.

They take a retreat from their target site. When Dark Lord returns from his full moon, walk in the surrounding forest and find his castle set ablaze, all captured on fire.

"Well my Viking lover we have no sex cave anymore."

"You do not worry, I want you to ride me anywhere you can."

***

Our Suki sisters are watching their evil site of evil on fire. When they notice men in black tactical unit uniforms returning to their vehicles after they cleared their den.

The sounds of a sniper rifle do not stop for a while before our twin sisters turn around and cancel tonight's plans they had made for the Dark Lord's castle.

"I wonder who were those men in daku?"

"I think some robber's gone home wrong."

"I like it."

"Why?"

"The robbery went south."

"Hahahaha."

But sisters laughing out loud went back to theirs government borrowed vehicle to scheme another way of finding to plot their murder plans further.

***

The time came for detective Simpleton to announce the course of change because he was in contact with local guilds who were working also in the background to eradicate Dark Lord's evil from their Island long ago they loved and killed for it.

Our hero Mage was going through planning in conversation to learn about new action points they take to rob the Bank of Sinners, making a point they would not tolerate aggression from the Crimson Lord.

"I think this goes beyond our imagination" Simon took a cup of morning coffee and walked away to see the sunrise.

"I do not believe we are imaging or this is reality. I cannot see beyond the point of reason fighting this mythical Lord who is the bringer of evil."

Mage takes his cup of coffee and joins Simon on the terrace overseeing the Lake view.

"I am in conversation with you. It is not NATO duty to oversee perverts and crooked politicians who are incapable of bringing war. I understand our unit duty is to prevent causes of war rather than become part of warfare."

"Yes, this guerilla conflict is to avoid civil war but they should take responsibility for what is their homeland rather than us."

Simon takes a last drink from his coffee cup and before he walks away to check on others, he says they are risking their lives here to the commanding officer.

***

The morning Suki sisters were having a full Crimson brunch in the local inn.

They booked a twin room before their next stop to investigate those strange men who did their best to rob them of their targets.

Aim and Fire

I

gnacius was thinking to ask Simon if he remembers the story of someone who jailed them for double homicide but he relaxed into the sofa seat and he was thinking long before today.

They arrived at the location before their Captain Mage and had to run area checks to learn about local surroundings.

It was a hot and sunny summer's afternoon.

They went out to a local pub drinking and met two beautiful Dutch women sitting near the river with maxi dresses revealing their legs closer to torso.

"What are you doing in such heat in the sun?"

"I can see you are laughing and having a great time."

"Well, we are relaxing." The girls laughed when Simon opened the conversation.

The two friends took time off and showed their girls the good time.

But when the night came they woke up in their beds naked and the lovers for the night went missing

They left in the morning for a full lunch menu and noticed outside their cafe a police presence and lots of local people standing close.

Ignacius said to Simon he believes it is old plastic washed ashore and the local community gathered to clean it up but Simon asked Ignacius to stop joking and he walked towards the crowd.

When he realized the crime scene victims, he froze in fear, his heart stopped.

Ignacius walked closer to him and rested his arm on Simon's shoulder to see closer. "OMG, I cannot believe it is two loose Dutch women who had a great orgy last night!"

"We better walk away." But when Simon finished his sentence, the thoughts his DNA found in their dead bodies will make him a criminal for life, made him desperate to wish he runs but he knew they needed the real culprit.

"I think we have a serial killer on the loose."

"I am feeling sick in my heart knowing how much pleasure we had they gave us and now seeing these rotten corpses fished out the water."

Our heroes did little, they knew the reasoning behind two murders they felt victims for. They walked away and left the hotel room early, taking their bedsheets with them.

"I think we are going camping tonight."

"I hate those bugs around us when it gets dark."

"They are better than prison food I guarantee you."

When they found a local forest near the motorway with an old barn left behind without use, they felt it would be great shelter to set their tents in and to set fire burning for their hotel bedding and boil hot soup.

The soup was boiling, Ignacius threw in a couple potatoes to let flames steam off from inside.

"When I find those pricks, I give them some metal."

"How do you know it is them and they are males?"

"I am sure it is sick bastards who killed our good night focks." Simon pushed around fire wood with his stick to let it burn even.

"I am sure they would give me a double blow job by the fire if they were still breathing."

"You are sick, Ignacius. Do you know that?"

"I just love life and good living."

The very next morning the headlines in local Sinbury papers wrote about two men wanted for a rape and murder of two female victims.

Simon and Ignacius tried to flee the city, but they apprehended them when one driver reported two hitchhikers looking similar to the suspects from the image of hotel CCTV pictures.

They did not resist making an arrest nor declined their saliva swab test to match found in victims' bodies.

While in the holding cell, Simon was thinking long and hard about who could have made them fall for the crimes they did not commit. But when the note passed under his door saying they must run to learn the truth today.

Simon made a knock on the door and asked if he could use the toilet before he could have more tea.

When the police station officer turned the key and pulled the door open, Simon hit his head on the door, throwing him backwards.

He stepped out and hit the officer's head with his boot.

"I am sorry mate but it will hurt me more than you."

He took his keys and opened Ignacius' cell door, letting him out and passing a police issued rifle.

"What took you so long?"

"I wonder what took Mage so long to post us a letter?"

"I cannot answer the question but we have a positive ID of the killer and we are taking police transport."

The little serial killer knew he would meet tonight machine versus machine.

They parked a police car two streets down the killer's house and booted doors open killing serial rapists in a single headshot from the picture they found inside an envelope our Detective Simpleton handed them in a local park.

His brains and blood particles splattered all over his family on their dinner table.

The moment they showed up, they left their crime scene, leaving no traces behind them.

When all was done Ignacius got drunk on home made whisky and he felt he cannot handle the night any further. Police arrested them driving around a river in a stolen jet ski wearing blue suits and neckties over their heads screaming at local water-way police. "Banzai!"

The next day our heroes were trying on their prison uniforms.

Their Captain was at the right altitude and speed flying to a private airport. He mixed with the world's most famous rock band to work as equipment assistant.

In the night our Simon was in his prison cell and he was thinking to himself. "She felt so good on him riding reverse cowgirl saying Sliht to him."

Ignacius in the opposite cell thought to himself they will have to tattoo tear drops on their cheeks.

The very next morning Ignacius told Simon they assigned him the D911 number and Simon told him he was an A113 prisoner.

They had a week before the final court trial and had good lessons about prison life.

It felt a little odd in gothic built prison barracks separated with narrow corridors as they walked, all inmates looking at them as if they did something wrong. Knowing they were in for a rape and murder trial since they had no proof left. They felt guilty.

The morning Ignacius was having his morning shower in a steam-packed showeroom with four facets near the toilet seat off the entrance. He sprays water on the inmate taking his clothes off.

He took a moment to brush water off his eyes to look at Ignacius and then he told his friends to stand watch at the door.

He took his top off and from his sleeve a small razer in between his fingertips.

"Now you are focked mate."

The other guys captured D911 by his armpits, taking him naked to the walls while a hot shower sprayed.

He kicked his feet away but the strength of the grip over his shoulders was too strong. He shouted but one inmate closed his mouth with the palm of his hand.

Simon walked to have his morning shower with his new friends to learn the door is held closed.

"What is the plug, ladies?"

He kicked doors open enough to see they are attempting to cut his friend.

With little thinking he ran in and his group of friends too.

They grabbed the men attempting to block the doors by their shoulders and did wrestle them down below the waist to smack their skulls to the walls.

Simon rushed forward and kicked the guy in his back from off his way who held a prison weapon.

Men lost their concentration allowing Ignacius to set his right arm free to punch the guy on his left on stomach while he was not letting go of his arm.

Ignacius used his left arm to twist around the arm that was holding him and with a light hip twist he broke it to pieces.

He pushed them together and kicked both aside as they slipped on the soap covered floor knocking their breath out of their lungs creating a feeling they cannot breathe in.

"Are you ok?"

"This one is a nasty piece of shat!"

"Guys, hold the doors till I place him where he belongs!" Then Simon picked him off the floor by his neck and pulled him to the toilet seat.

"I was only teaching our rookie a lesson."

Simon took no time listening to him beg for mercy and flipped him overhead, drowning his head in the toilet feces.

"I think your foul mouth belongs here." Simon was thinking while he was gasping for air in the dirt.

***

When Ignacius finished telling his prison story it amazed Mage about their prison school.

"It sounds a little like a life Ignacius."

"I would not call it but it was like no other experience I felt."

"You guys try easy next time and no slapping random asses while on a mission no matter how much honey you think you will find inside."

"Yes, the sex was great but who could tell it was a serial psychopath who did kill them after the girls left our bedroom before their morning flight."

"You should keep your battleship mast to yourself. We focus on mission we could go home and then maybe I let you have some because you and Simon are like sex addicts."

Simon walks with a smile. "We may be addicts but who loves a good possy they can find."

Their conversation stops when our Detective Simpleton is reporting good news.

Do you like Koto flavour?

Th
he morning Dark Lord was drinking his coffee he leaned on his chair and was looking through Dark Castle out in blue skies.

The one faithful morning he remembers his youth how he and his schoolmates visited His Excellency Blond's home.

They were school friends who were upper classmates to young Blond. They saw Blond in his house and they played games on his game station.

His friends were sitting in the lounge shouting and running across fields of mushrooms in a video game attempting to avoid obstacles to save the princess in time he said he needed to take a leak.

Young Blond was sitting in a corner feeling isolated from his school friends with dark eyelids from school work.

Dark Lord walks in a corridor and walks towards the restroom to see a divorced homemaker preparing snacks for her son's upperclassmen.

Young Lord looks at her and feels the temptation to have the desert she has early.

He walks up to her and places his arm down her waist with others squeezing her butt.

"Did your Mr. Blond leaves you because you are not good enough to look after his rejects?"

She speaks nothing but licks her lips and concentrates, completing her dessert.

He feels more tempted to open her up for no reason and pushes her waist closer to the kitchen top where she is standing.

He rubs his groin closer to her and pulls her top down halfway, revealing her chest and bra she is wearing.

"I told you in the name of my royal household to kneel before me and beg for redemption you give me."

She kneels on her knees with her hands shaking in panic to avoid any trouble with her son because her husband abandoned them long ago they cannot afford the trouble.

He spits down the sink and tells her to open his zip and let her know what she will need to do next so she could serve her country.

She strokes her hand down his waist and takes out the young Dark Lord's pride and joy, stroking it a couple times before she places it in her mouth.

When upperclassmen get tired and leave a joystick to another kid, he could see what desert is taking so long he walks in the kitchen seeing his country's future lord spreading open a homemaker on the kitchen counter top.

Her legs open and wrapped around his Dark Lord, keeping her mouth shut and kissing his neck with her plain gaze at his classmate.

"I will finish it soon, there is nothing to stare at."

The Dark Lord tells another kid who continues walking in the restroom to look in a mirror, pick between his teeth and check his breath after he spits in the sink.

He walks out and he can see the young Dark Lord finished spreading his seed between her.

His classmate walks up to her and asks his Dark Lord to play console in another room because the pause will not last long.

He decided he had not done it from behind yet and would like to practice it while she is fit for it.

He pulls her arm and tells her to bend over. He could see her taking off her underwear. He could observe her cleaning the fluids dripping from her with it he could be sure the passage is clean enough to start over.

She does as he says and when children are done playing, they wish good bye to each other thanking for hospitality waves goodbye before leaving the household.

***

When our Mage had a positive message over concealed radio transmission from Mr. Simpleton, they left early in the morning to seek justice for the island they sought to leave.

They drove in black four wheel drive car made bulletproof pass buildings made a century ago but avoided world war bombs.

They were checking their assault rifles for cartridges and counting bullets before the eventual destination.

Mage was thinking to himself why Detective Simpleton told him to leave Dark Lord to be because four archangels said to him they will open seven gates under heaven to break the seal they kept locked from us and heaven itself the justice serves.

He thought the reasoning is unusual and why some sort of force should be able to devour the belly of the beast because the Blond or Dark Lord has an appetite for pure insanity of evil but who could cut them dead so easily.

With little time to think they reached their site and Simon drove up the stairs, the Bank of Sinisters forcing passersby to run to the side watching black SUV forcing its way to the Nation's Bank.

Simon jumped outside, but he was not wearing his black Swiss style tactical gear. He was wearing royal crimson family attire with a printed paper mask of the Dark Lord, the same dress code applied to Mage and Ignacius. When passersby thought they charged their own national bank shooting live rounds in bank security in front of them.

They did wear medals and royal crests it was difficult to say it was not the royal crimson family taking up violence on the street.

The team charged the Bank of Sinisters, shooting security guards down, avoiding leaving anybody breathing able to use firearms.

They hit the blond lady's head over the counter because she was too slow to tell them where the key to the safe was.

Simon took his handgun and forced her throat, explaining to her he will shoot it better than from his testicles.

She had a tear in her eyes and pointed her finger to the draw where they found the vault master key.

Simon said thank you to the blond lady. "We will fock later once I cash my check in darling."

Our heroes were taking a corridor to the vault when Simon saw passing him by a Bank Manager with his name badge saying Carl Pirdila.

He made a roundhouse kick and cracked his skull to the wall.

"Take this satanic manager."

When our heroes run outside holding top secret government documents, money, crown jewelry and digital stock market keys plus a couple gold bars, they realize they are surrounded by an incoming police force.

The boot of their black SUV opened over seeing police vehicles towards them but the grandmother who looked alike stood up pushing her tired hairy leg out of the boot wearing a royal family dress.

She stood up, looking at speeding police vehicles towards her, gave a good stretch to her back from side to side and picked up her rocket launcher.

She took the safety lid off, aimed and fired at police carnage of transport.

Around the corner a white van started its engine and with screeching wheels made a round turn from the parking space.

Two window cleaners from the van opened their side doors with the big motto logo We Clean it for U, ahead of the burning and tilted police transport and waved their hands at our heroes.

The cosplay of the royal family ran inside their transport and drove off.

"Blast, this skirt waist is not mine." He pulled the paper mask off and opened a bottle of lager.

"Yes Detective Simpleton, I think skirts and dresses never suited you."

They all laughed.

"But I am sure I gave them a big one."

Once they lost their stolen transport, they sat in Detectives Simpleton's wide car and drove to a pub called Pig Pit to have their well deserved drinks.

After a few drinks they meet a couple cute girls talking about Disco down the road from where they are.

"Oh, you are Detective Mr. Simpleton. We are sure we will meet one."

Two cute Japanese girls laughed.

"What a coincidence, we were planning to cut our business trip short before we head back home to Japan but I think we are ok to have a delightful dance."

"I am sure my nephews would be more than happy to escort you."

Our Detective Simpleton pours the last pint of lager to his mouth and leaves home to watch tomorrow's news about four archangels promised they sent from the heavens to save our earth.

Bob and Dylan were standing in the corner and smiling at our young heroes, thinking they would meet excellent partners for tonight.

They waved their hands, smiling.

"Good luck lads! We think we will stay here for a few more drinks before we crawl back to our beds."

Ignacius walks to two girls to say he learned about them from his uncle Simpleton.

"I think my uncle said we are free to escort you to the disco tonight in case there are no good dance partners."

"Yeh, I think he mentioned something."

Nami looks at her sister and smiles, who is looking at their drinks menu.

Simon is so drunk he stumbles on Ignacius' shoulder, holding a cocktail of whiskey and energy drink, looking to learn the conversation.

"We must enjoy tonight because stargazing told me it is the right tonight."

Our girls laughed and offered him a few more drinks before they would see him fit, have them out on a date tonight.

"Ok, guys, you know what I told you about drinking and dating beautiful women?"

"Roger that, Captain Crimson, but we're done for tonight?"

"Yeah, it is true and I think I am ok to see you out of this pub before you vomit here."

They left for the dance floor to see a guest DJ Kuku Kola.

The place was so great and music was swinging the atmosphere well they started dancing under the disco floor.

"I think this tune beats harder than a police officer when you are drunk on the floor."

"I think this beats harder than grandmother's pain killers."

"No! I think it beats harder than a drunk father from the bar."

"Nope. It beats harder than pandemia."

Do you say Sakai?

T

he team loaded their assault rifles and wore full assault gear Simon Says said to them before the last mission together.

"Tonight we load some timber and it will be tonight they will remember."

The team left seeking revenge for the entire nation with only two faithful nationals who escaped their prison.

Our Detective Simpleton was home relaxing because he knew it would shake the nation about justice served before Crimson King and his country were taken for ransom.

"You hear us guys, we take no prisoners and kiss them hard with our slugs."

"Yes, we fock them hard like our first and last love."

"Roger, we closed our radio channel. We start work."

The Tvart Way 10 had an urgent office meeting they called Snake, where all official heads of government had to complete strategic planning to resolve the crisis their nation experienced after their Bank of Sinisters lost state secrets, including valuable assets.

The time outside our Bob and Dylan the Demolition Brothers cut the throats of a couple police officers standing guard at the rear post.

"We are like a couple cut throats."

"Yeh and a very low rent."

Meanwhile, once blood did not finish leaking out officers' throats, the major assault team made their way to the main entrance because time was the key to essence in operation the Black Edge they were preparing in the former abandoned military facility the Black Site.

Once they stormed into the building, Bob dropped a bag of plastic explosions close to the electric generator for the team captain to detonate it and turn off the power supply, creating a blackout.

When they opened the last door and murdered the last guards, they shot dead all the secretaries of Crimson state.

"What do we do with this woman?"

Simon Says without further talk fired two slugs in His Excellency Blond chest.

"You give her a good fock."

When Mage walks in to inform he has secured the escape route perimeter, he can see Simon sitting in the highest ranked government officials chair smoking a cigar. Ignacius is pumping his mast through the open zip in His Excellency wife between her spread while she is rubbing her arms on his flag vest and kissing his neck.

"You guys make me sick every time I let you take control."

He splashes her blood and part of brains over Ignacius' face.

"I was about to do her in. Simon said she is a great joy ride."

"Well, I finished for you. You can close your zipper or if you love corpses go ahead while we head home."

He stood up, zipped his crotch and spat down. "I think we are done here."

Simon places his cigar and picks up his CAR 15 make rifle.

"She was just a joy ride, let's move on, brothers. We need a real future to catch."

"I would rather live a moment than think anything is greater."

"Well said Ignacius."

"Thank you, our Captain."

He saluted our Mage. And they took an escape route to take cover and lie low before Detective four archangels will make a miracle they were waiting for.

***

The Dark Lord in his Dark Castle just finished his phone call listening to his kingdom politicians getting murdered by well prepared assailants with unknown origins to the police force.

He places his phone down and takes a deep breath, letting his air out, and closes his eyes.

"At least Blond slat made me two kids."

He opens his mini bar and takes a bottle of rum to celebrate the dead weak and strong who will survive.

But it felt like time had stopped and the Deja Vu moment made him think something was not right.

He can see dark smoke coming from all gaps of windows and doors, making his hand shake, feeling faint legs.

He cannot move or scream at his guard to save him from fire to learn now in the middle of his dark hall is a standing black figure in dark steel armour looking at him.

"You are the one who calls himself the supreme commander?" The hard voice spoke to him.

But before Dark Lord of Crimson Nation could open his jaw to let sound out.

'I see you are a weakling not worth your titles nor life you. Die."

Grand Duke, who traveled from stones of time in his sleep from the illustrious past of Grand Duke's Kingdom, closed his arm the moment he spelled Die.

He left the Dark Lord a splatter of blood covering every corner of Crimson Nation Dark Hall.

***

The very next morning the young Viking Princess was packing her bags to take the first flight back home and on the table were the Morning Nation newspaper.

The headlines were about acts of terrorism taking lives of innocent His Excellency family and his government secretaries suspects related to the day before armed robbery of the National Bank. With most shocking news our Crimson Lord turns ill and became diseased, medics confirmed morning after act of terrorism.

She just packed her bags and took black taxi to a major airport because she felt there was no more fun to play with in her desires.

She thought on her way to the airport which nation's lord would be great next sex toy.

The taxi driver packed her luggage on a trolley, and she paid him a tip.

She looked at boarding time and walked to powder her makeup fresh before she boarded her business class seat back to Viking Kingdom.

The ladies' lounge restrooms were clean and full of fresh odour, to see an oriental girl cleaning toilet seats. She felt disgusted that she was sucking on her candy in her lips while brushing the floor.

"Could you leave, I prefer private time in the ladies room."

"Apologies." She made a light bow and started walking away.

"But you die." Nami said and spit in her neck vocal cords light poison needle.

Yami walked out from the occupied cabin and closed her mouth with tissue pulling her inside.

The time came a few hours later for her driver to pick his Princess but he learned she did not board her flight back home, he found only her luggage sent home.

But when he picked up her luggage, the airport guard dog started barking at him and security had to open her bags, finder her cut in pieces covered in plastic.

Yami and Nami landed in the same flight watching how their faces turned pale watching a scene from a horror movie.

"They can build her back to a stone statue."

"Yep. It will last longer than her sick desires to fock every nobleman she can find."

They took a taxi and continued to their hotel to close their business deal.

***

Mage and his team were giving their last goodbyes before they boarded the fishing boat, taking them back to safety after their hardship completing their mission they got from Detective Simpleton.

Bob and Dylan were standing tall and firm, proud after participating in NATO Black Site camp training helped them assist seasoned soldiers in combat operations.

"We learned so much from you, Simon. The lessons we took on how to use sharps and how to keep it. We are happy you advised us and trained how to store poison on your sleeve the time we need it oiled on blades we use to make an escape."

"No worries lads. I was happy you learned rather than rot in Crimson Prison."

"Ok. We're done talking, the time is for us to go."

But out of nowhere Simon's feet began to smoke in black smoke engulfing him in black fire and dark clouds covered in black rain pulling Simon out of space through a black narrow corridor he can hear medical equipment beeping and feeling faint light coming through eyelids.

About Author

He grew up in the Lithuanian post soviet era and was educated about art and design in London.

He was learning from design masters and travelled the world.

www.ingramcontent.com/pod-product-compliance
Lightning Source LLC
Chambersburg PA
CBHW061710130726
47996CB00006B/2249